A BAN

The Big Gold Robbery

· ERROL LLOYD ·

Illustrated by
The Author

HEINEMANN · LONDON

First published in Great Britain 1993
by William Heinemann Ltd
an imprint of Reed Consumer Books Ltd
Michelin House, 81 Fulham Road, London SW3 6RB

AUCKLAND MELBOURNE SINGAPORE TORONTO

ISBN 0 434 96267 8

Printed in Italy by Olivotto

A school pack of Banana Books 55-60
is available from
Heinemann Educational Books
ISBN 0 435 00109 4

Chapter 1

It was Kelly's mum's birthday, and he and the gang were searching for a present for her.

Sasha suggested they try the local market and they were heading in that direction when they spotted the crowd.

They swung round their bikes and joined the people gathered around a street vendor.

'Ten years ago,' he was saying, 'there was the biggest gold robbery in history. Ten million pounds' worth of gold was stolen. The police found the robbers, but they never found the gold. Now, ladies and gentlemen, here in front of your very eyes is some of the finest jewellery in the world: signet rings, friendship rings, pendants, necklaces, sweetheart tags. . .'

The man paused for breath allowing the crowd, which was getting bigger by the minute, to take in what he had said.

'Watch out for the police,' he

announced. 'When they come one way I go the other . . .'

He took a necklace and held it up for the crowd to see.

'In the shops a piece looking just like this sells for three hundred pounds. Now I'm not asking three hundreds pounds. I'm not asking two hundred pounds. I'm not even asking for fifty pounds.' And he clapped his hands. 'Just give me a fiver each and they're yours.'

He didn't have to wait long. A man in a blue bomber jacket thrust a ten pound note in his hand, snapped up two chains and disappeared.

That started the ball rolling and soon people were fighting to buy these bargains.

After he had served a dozen people the man in the blue bomber jacket came back and whispered something to him. Quick as a flash, he snatched up the suitcase and they darted down the steps to the underground station. The crowd scattered in all directions.

The gang were leaving too when they saw a policeman coming down the road. He was heading straight towards them.

Chapter 2

THE GANG RECOGNISED the policeman as P.C. Phillips, who had been on duty when they had helped to catch some bicycle thieves a few weeks earlier.

'Now then kids,' said P.C. Phillips. 'What are you all up to, eh? I hope you are not playing detectives again. Remember, catching crooks is a job for the police.'

'We were just watching,' said Sasha.

'That man was selling jewellery made from stolen gold,' said Kelly.

'And that means people were buying stolen goods,' said Tunde.

'I see you fell for it too,' said P.C. Phillips. 'Just like the people who bought the jewellery!'

'Then why did the people all run away when they saw you coming if they weren't buying stolen goods?' asked Michael.

'They only *thought* they were buying stolen goods,' P.C. Phillips replied. 'You see, that jewellery is only gold-plated costume jewellery. It's made from cheap base metal with a thin layer of gold on the outside.'

'But he said it was gold,' said Tara.

'You only imagined he said it was gold, just like all those people who bought the jewellery,' explained P.C. Phillips.

'Because he talks about the gold robbery, people thinks he's selling jewellery made from the stolen gold. But he never actually says it's made from gold. Not if you listen carefully. It's just an old confidence trick.'

'But why did he say that it's the same as the jewellery in the shops which costs £300?' said Kelly.

'He only says that his jewellery *looks*

like the jewellery in the shops. And that's quite true. They look exactly alike, but while the jewellery in the shops is made from solid gold, his is imitation,' explained P.C. Phillips.

'If he wasn't doing anything wrong, why did he keep running off when he thought the police were coming?' asked Nadine.

'That was just another way of convincing people that he was selling stolen gold. When a real policeman comes along it's even more convincing! Small time con men they may be, but they have a street licence to sell,' went on P.C. Phillips. 'The costume jewellery they sell for £5 is good value for money. I bought one of their necklaces for my wife and she really liked it. Well I'll be on my way,' he said, 'and remember, not all that glitters is gold!'

Chapter 3

P.C. PHILLIPS WAS hardly out of sight before the vendor was in operation again.

This time Kelly pulled out his £5 note and quickly bought a necklace.

'Just the thing for Mum's birthday,' he said.

Then he and the rest of the gang mounted their bikes and rode back to the basement headquarters of the BRAT club. (BRAT stands for Bicycle Riders' Action Team.)

They decided to meet at ten o'clock the next morning to go and look at some Mountain Bikes.

When Kelly reached home that evening he headed straight for his room and took out the necklace. He wrapped it neatly in gift paper and wrote on a birthday card: To Mum with love from Kelly.

Soon he heard a key in the front door. It was Kelly's dad. He also had a present for Kelly's mum, and a huge delicious-looking birthday cake. They decided to play a trick on Mum. They pretended that they had forgotten about her birthday. After dinner when Kelly's dad came back from the kitchen with the coffee, it was the signal for Kelly to turn off the lights. And there was the birthday cake, all lit up with pink candles. They sang 'Happy Birthday' and Kelly's Mum shrieked with delight. 'You rotters!' she said. 'And I thought you had both forgotten!' She was really pleased when she opened the presents. 'Thanks Kelly,' she said, when she saw the necklace. 'It's lovely. I'll stop in at the jeweller on my way to work and ask him to fit my locket onto the chain.'

Chapter 4

When his mum and dad left for work the next morning, Kelly cycled to the BRAT Club. The other members were already there.

As he cycled into the yard, Mrs. King from the flat above called out to Kelly:

'Kelly! Your mum's on the phone for you!'

'Coming!' Kelly shouted.

Mrs. King allowed the BRAT members to receive emergency calls on her phone. *Why on earth did his mother want to talk to him now* he wondered.

'Hello, Mum,' he said.

'I'm ringing about the chain you gave me,' said Mum. 'When I took it to the jeweller, he examined it and said it was real gold.'

'Real gold!' repeated Kelly.

'According to the jeweller that necklace is worth over £300! We'll have to take it back to the shop where you bought it,' said his mum.

'But you can't. I bought it from a man in the street,' said Kelly.

'Look, Kelly, I have to go now, but when I get home I'll want a better explanation than that!'

'But Mum . . .'

The phone went dead.

Kelly thanked Mrs. King and hurried back to join the gang.

'It's real!' he shouted.

'What's real?' asked Tunde.

'The necklace I bought for Mum, yesterday,' he said. 'It's real gold. A jeweller told my mum and she rang to find out where I got it.'

'I can't believe it!' said Nadine.

'If the gold is real, then the men selling it were telling the truth,' said Tunde. 'They must be the gold robbers.'

'We'd better phone the police,' said Sasha.

They had a difficult time trying to convince the police that a necklace they had bought for £5 from a street vendor was in fact worth £300.

'They say we must bring in the necklace with a £5 receipt from the street vendor. They also want a letter from the jeweller valuing the jewellery at £300,' said Tunde.

Chapter 5

THE GANG WERE a bit unsure of what to do next, but they found themselves riding towards the underground station where they had bought the necklace.

The same two men were there, hard at work: 'Ten years ago was the greatest gold robbery in history . . .'

The gang knew without asking that the vendor was not going to write out a receipt for the jewellery. So they decided to spy on the men from a safe distance, and then make a report to the police when they had some hard information.

They had brought their walkie-talkies with them so they could shadow the men without the risk of getting too close.

It took the men half an hour to sell all their jewellery and move off down the street.

The gang decided to split up into three pairs taking it in turn to watch the men. They kept in touch by sending messages to each other over the walkie-talkie system.

Before long, an urgent message came through from Sasha: 'Suspects have entered antique shop in Grafton Terrace. Over.'

'Stay where you are,' said Tunde, 'and keep an eye on them. We'll all meet at the corner of Grafton Terrace in three minutes. Over and out.'

The gang met and watched the antique shop with a mixture of excitement and curiosity. They watched as passers-by entered the shop and later left clutching their purchases.

'It seems like a normal shop,' said Tara.

'It could be a cover for something else,' warned Tunde.

'Let's go in and pretend to be customers looking for bargains,' suggested Kelly.

'Best if only two go in,' said Tunde. 'At any hint of danger they can report back on the walkie-talkie.'

'I'll go,' volunteered Kelly.

'I'll go too,' added Sasha. She was determined that the boys shouldn't get to do all the exciting bits.

Chapter 6

As Kelly and Sasha pushed the door open, a loud chime announced their arrival.

To their surprise no one was in sight.

They had a quick look around. There were pianos, dusty second-hand books, gramophone records, broken lamps, tables, desks and all kinds of bric-a-brac.

Antique paintings lined the wall beside the narrow staircase. A fluffy tabby cat lay asleep in an armchair.

Presently they heard voices coming from the rear of the shop and two familiar figures emerged from behind a beaded curtain.

They recognised the man in front as the street vendor. He was lugging a heavy suitcase. He was followed by his partner.

'What do you want?' he inquired in a gruff voice.

'We just want to have a look round to see what you've got,' blurted out Kelly.

'Well make it fast,' said the man. 'We ain't got time for a bunch of kids with only peanuts to spend.'

'We're closing soon,' called the second man. 'I'll give you kids just five minutes.'

'Let's look upstairs,' whispered Kelly to Sasha, and they quickly mounted the creaking staircase.

He and Sasha crossed the landing and went into a room filled with big old furniture.

'The five minutes are nearly up,' whispered Sasha.

'OK, let's go,' nodded Kelly. They were heading back to the staircase, when the door chime announced the entry of a new customer.

'OK fellows, just stay right where you are and no one is gonna get hurt,' said a rough voice downstairs to the vendor and his mate.

Kelly and Sasha froze.

'What you got in that suitcase?' they heard the strange voice demand.

'Just some cheap costume jewellery,'

said the vendor. 'Nothing that you fellows would be interested in.'

'We'll soon find out,' came the reply.

'Pheeew,' they heard the stranger whistle as he opened the suitcase. 'You boys haven't been laying your grubby hands on our gold, have you?'

'Take it easy,' the street vendor replied. 'We don't know what you're talking about, do we Bill?' he added, turning to his mate.

'Well, I'm Ronnie Buster and my mate here is Harry "Bone Crusher" Miller. We've just finished a ten year stretch for a certain gold robbery and we're here to collect the loot.'

'You mean you did the big robbery where they captured the robbers but never found the gold . . .'

'Not until you found it that is,' said Ronnie menacingly.

'We don't know nothing about no gold,' protested the vendor. 'All we found was some jewellery hidden in a cupboard. We figured it was cheap costume jewellery and we been selling it for a fiver a piece.'

'Hear that, Bone Crusher?' said Ronnie. 'They've been flogging our stuff for a fiver. That ain't polite.'

'Oh, so you thought it was cheap gold plate did you?' growled Bone Crusher.

'Well, I'll let you into a little secret. That jewellery was solid gold. You wouldn't expect us to go round selling gold bars now, would you? So we melted some of it down, didn't we, Ronnie?'

'Yea. We ain't stupid,' said Ronnie. 'Let's tie 'em up and check upstairs if they've found the bars too.'

Sasha and Kelly looked round for somewhere to hide. The only place was an old brass bed covered with a thick patchwork quilt. They slipped under the quilt and lay as still as possible.

Chapter 7

THE STAIRCASE CREAKED louder and louder as Ronnie and Bone Crusher made their way upstairs. They entered the room where Sasha and Kelly were hiding.

'Now where was it we bricked up the lolly?' asked Ronnie.

'I reckon it's over there,' answered Bone Crusher, pointing in the direction of the brass bed. 'We'll have to shift that bed out of the way.'

They grabbed either side of the bed.

'Weighs a bloomin' ton,' said Ronnie.

'My granny used to have one of these,' said Bone Crusher, panting for breath.

'They don't make 'em like this any

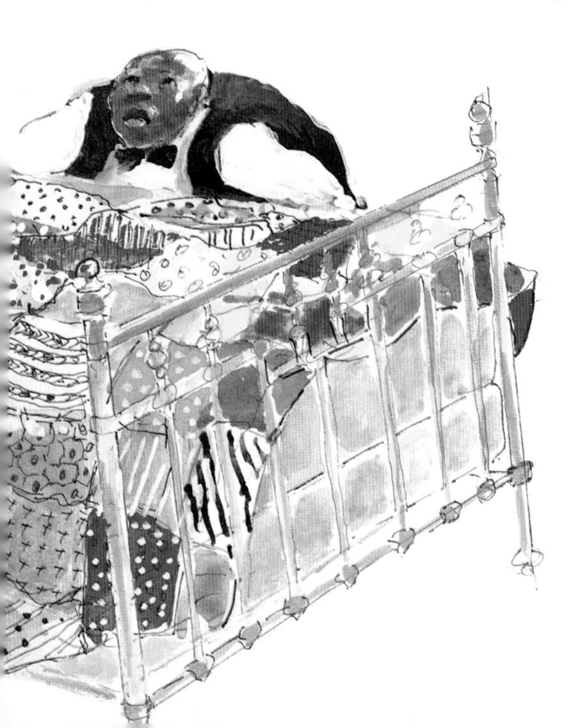

more,' exclaimed Ronnie.

Once the bed was moved, they examined the wall more closely.

'This is the spot alright,' said Harry. 'See, the secret markings are still there.'

Kelly and Sasha lay motionless as they heard the two men hack away at the wall with a hammer and pickaxe.

Then, suddenly the noise ceased.

'Is the loot still there?' asked Bone Crusher anxiously.

'Every single bar!' came the reply. 'Just look at 'em. Have you ever seen anything more beautiful?'

And they began to laugh.

'I tell you what,' said Ronnie. 'I'm gonna go and fetch the transit van to shift this lot. I shouldn't be away more than half an hour. You stay outside the shop and make sure nobody gets in. And don't forget to put the CLOSED sign on the door.'

Kelly and Sasha breathed a sigh of relief as they heard the two men going down the stairs and the bell ring as the shop door slammed shut.

'Quick, we have no time to spare,' said Kelly as he and Sasha came out from under the bedcover.

They went to the top of the stairs and peeped down. The enormous frame of Bone Crusher was guarding the front door.

'There's no way we can get out now,' said Sasha.

Then Kelly remembered the walkie-talkie.

They went over to the rear window and tried to make contact with the gang.

'Receiving you loud and clear. What took you so long? Over,' said Tunde crossly.

'Can't explain now,' said Kelly. 'But we've found the gold.'

'You're kidding,' said Tunde. 'Over.'

'Just what we figured you'd say,' said Kelly. 'But you must get to the police right away. We can't leave. One of the robbers is guarding the front door. Over.'

'The police won't believe us without proof,' said Tunde.

'There's only one thing to do,' said Kelly. 'We must get a bar of the stolen gold to the police station. They can't argue about that can they? We'll lower it down through the back window. Over and out.'

Then he made his way through the opening in the wall into the room full of gold. Carefully he carried one of the bars over to where Sasha was waiting with a length of rope.

Meanwhile the other members of the gang had gathered in the deserted cobbled lane at the back of the shop. Sasha secured the gold bar firmly with the rope and she and Kelly gently lowered it into the

waiting hands of Michael below.

'Straight to the police,' said Tunde. 'And tell them to get here as fast as they can.'

Michael put the gold bar in his backpack and mounted his bike.

'Wait for me,' called Nadine, speeding behind him.

Chapter 8

Barely ten minutes later, a line of blue police uniforms could be seen snaking its way up the lane at the back. They had a ladder with them, and four burly policemen clambered up and eased themselves through the window into the showroom.

At the same time a van drew up at the front of the shop.

'He's back!' whispered Kelly.

Sasha and Kelly darted under the bedcover and the policemen hid behind the door leading into the showroom.

The robbers entered the showroom and headed for the room with the gold. There was a brief scuffle followed by the words:

'You're under arrest.'

Kelly and Sasha breathed a sigh of relief as they left their hiding place just in time to see the robbers being led away.

They followed the police downstairs to where the two street vendors were tied up. The police cut the ropes binding their

hands, and took them away for questioning.

After all the excitement had died down the gang learned that they were to receive a reward from the company that had insured the gold. And Kelly was allowed to keep the gold necklace he had bought

for his mum.

On their way home the gang stopped at the Sports Shop to admire the Mountain Bikes. They knew exactly what they were going to do with the reward money!